# POLICE CAT

## Enid Hinkes

### Illustrated by Wendy Rasmussen

NOODLES

Albert Whitman & Company
Morton Grove, Illinois

To my husband, Bill, and to Anna.—E.H.

To Doris—my friend, colleague,
and mentor.—W.R.

Library of Congress Cataloging-in-Publication Data

Hinkes, Enid.
Police cat / written by Enid Hinkes ; illustrated by Wendy Rasmussen.
p. cm.
Summary: Noodles the cat takes his responsibilities very seriously, keeping the police station
and neighborhood safe and free from rats, but he is not an official member of the police
department until after he performs a heroic rescue.
ISBN: 978-0-8075-5758-7 (hardcover)
ISBN: 978-0-8075-5759-4 (paperback)
1. Cats—Juvenile fiction. [1. Cats—Fiction. 2. Police—Fiction. 3. Heroes—Fiction.]
I. Rasmussen, Wendy, 1952- ill. II. Title.
PZ10.3.H577Po 2005 [E]—dc22 2004018606

The design is by Wendy Rasmussen and Carol Gildar.

For more information about Albert Whitman & Company,
please visit our web site at www.albertwhitman.com.

There are many cats who do not care if the city is taken over by rats.

At night, when the rats come out, you will find those cats in warm houses, sleeping on pillows and eating food that comes out of little cans . . . or hanging out in alleys, meowing and keeping everyone awake.

But not Noodles. He was not that kind of cat.

Noodles worked out of the Third District Police Station.

Every night at eleven o'clock—2300 hours in police time—
Noodles left the station and went on patrol.

He chased away the rats who hung around the garbage cans.

He checked around the basements of houses to make sure
that rats were not sneaking in through holes or broken windows.
He went up and down the streets and alleys of the city,
keeping it safe for the children asleep in their beds.

Every morning, when Noodles returned to the police station, he walked past a police car, called the K-9 cruiser, where Truman the police dog sat. Truman jumped up and down and barked. He was always trying to get out of the car to chase Noodles.

Noodles did not pay any attention to the ill-mannered dog. "No dignity," he thought, "and useless. He probably never caught a rat in his life. Police dogs are nothing but squirrel chasers."

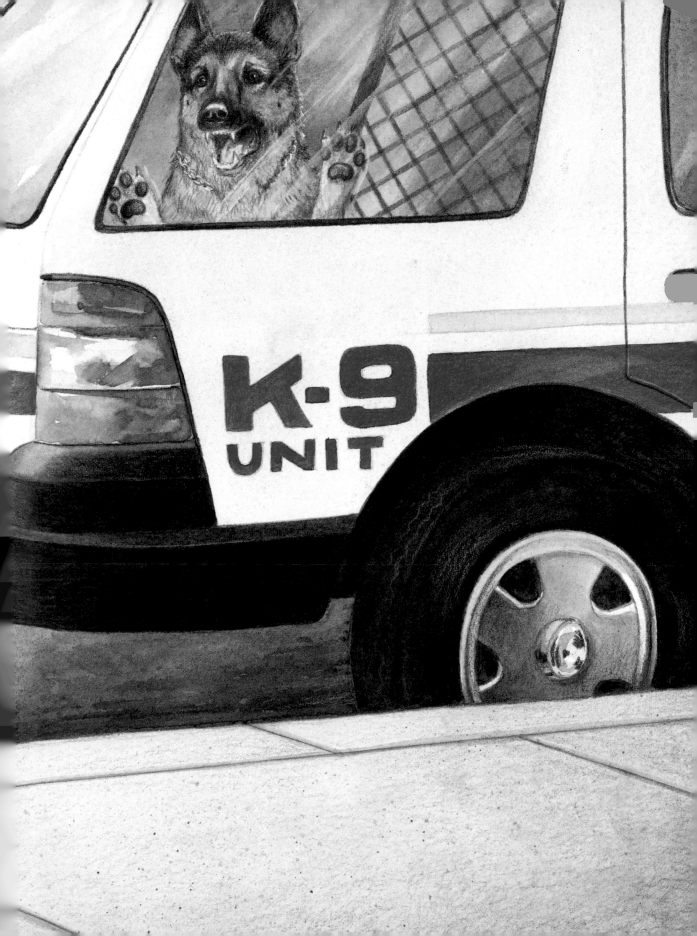

Noodles meowed and scratched at the station house door.
Sergeant Bowser, the desk sergeant, let him in. Then Noodles
curled up to go to sleep in a box underneath a desk where the
Commander could not see him.

"Unauthorized!" shouted the Commander whenever he
caught Noodles inside the station. Then he would order the
officers to throw Noodles out.

Because even though Noodles was the best rat-chaser in
the city, he was not an official member of the Metropolitan
Police Department.

The police department had K-9 units for dogs—they
even got special police cars and collars—but nothing for cats.
Not that any self-respecting cat would wear a collar.

Early one morning, Noodles was on his way back to the station when he saw a pack of rats scamper out through a broken basement window and run down the alley.

"Mischief is afoot," he thought.

Noodles climbed through the broken window into the basement. He smelled smoke. He saw flames in one corner. The rats had chewed a wire and started a fire.

Noodles had to warn the people in the house!

He hurried up the
stairs. At the top was a closed
door. Noodles had watched the officers at
the station turn knobs to open doors, but he had
never opened a door by himself. Now he knew he had to try.
He stood on his hind legs and stretched his front paws up.
He could barely reach the doorknob. He stepped back, jumped up,
and grabbed the knob. But his paws couldn't hold onto
the smooth surface, and he fell back down.
The fire was spreading.

He tried again, jumping and grabbing the doorknob. This time he placed his feet on the door and hung on, twisting and turning as hard as he could. The door opened!

He raced through the house. He saw an open door and dashed in. There were two girls—Anna and Sophie—sound asleep.

Noodles was not a cat who usually made a lot of noise, but he started to meow as loud as he could. When the girls didn't wake up, he jumped on Anna's bed and nudged the little girl's face with his paw. It worked! At last she opened her eyes. "Oh," she said, "a cat!"

Noodles leapt to the next bed where her sister was sleeping. He meowed again. This time, he had help. "Wake up, Sophie," said Anna. "There's a cat in here. And . . . something smells funny!"

Sophie sat up right away. "It's smoke!"

The girls ran to wake their mom and dad.
There was no time to call 911. Everyone rushed out
of the burning house with Noodles leading the way.
They were safe!

The K-9 car was coming down the street.
Sophie and Anna's parents flagged it down.

"Our house is on fire!" their dad shouted.
The officer in the car called for help.

The fire engines soon pulled up, followed by more police cars and a television camera truck.

Noodles saw that his work was done. It had been a long night, and he was looking forward to curling up in his box under the desk at the station. As he walked by the K-9 car, Truman leapt out and barked at him.

"No dignity," thought Noodles, "and useless."

Truman kept barking, even after Noodles was out of sight. He barked so loudly that the firemen could barely hear the fire chief's orders. Everyone looked at Truman.

"He must be the dog that woke the family up!" a reporter shouted.

"I thought it was a cat that saved them," another reporter said.

But no one listened. They had already gathered around Truman, petting him and taking his picture.

Then the television cameras were filming Truman! As Truman sat there barking, a reporter said:

"This dog is a hero. Like the hard-working and dedicated member of the police force that he is, he discovered the fire and saved four lives!"

The next morning the newspaper headlines read, "Dog Hero Saves the Day!" Truman loved the attention the officers gave him. He barked and wagged his tail, especially when someone gave him a dog biscuit.

"Gloryhound," thought Noodles.

Noodles had just settled in for a catnap when he noticed two girls coming into the station, followed by their parents. It was the family from last night!

"Excuse me, sir," Anna said to the Commander. "There has been a mistake. The newspapers reported that a dog rescued us last night. But it wasn't a dog. It was a cat—a small brown-and-black-striped cat with big ears."

"That's Noodles!" exclaimed Sergeant Bowser.

"Not that unauthorized cat," grumbled the Commander.

That afternoon the Mayor, the Chief of Police, and television and newspaper reporters arrived.

Noodles was given a Hero-of-the-City Award, a year's supply of canned cat food (which he donated to the animal shelter), a special door to enter the police station, an official police box to sleep in, and most important of all—

Noodles was now an official Metropolitan Police Department Cat! He posed in his new uniform and hat for his official photograph.

After everyone left, he took off his uniform. A cat can't chase rats with a tie on. He kept the hat on so he could show off to Truman, but he lost it that night while answering a 911 call with his fellow officers. That was okay. He was a Metropolitan Police Cat, and he had a job to do.

And Noodles is still out doing his job every night,
protecting you and all the other children.